Melanin Brown
DISCOVERS AMERICA

www.mascotbooks.com

Melanin Brown Discovers America

For more information, please contact:
Mascot Books
620 Herndon Parkway, Suite 320
Herndon, VA 20170
info@mascotbooks.com

Library of Congress Control Number: 2020916712

CPSIA Code: PRV1220A

ISBN-13: 978-1-64543-397-2

Printed in the United States

Melanin Brown
DISCOVERS AMERICA

**CANDICE
DAVIS**

Illustrated by
**BENEDICTA
BUATSIE**

This book is dedicated to my courageous mother, Jackie, and to all the young ladies and gentlemen who have ever been bullied. You are not alone, and you are valued.

I would also like to thank the National Museum of African American History and Culture for their help and inspiration. This book wouldn't be the same without them.

Contents

CHAPTER 1

Mom & Melanin

I QUICKLY FINISH TAKING the twists out of my hair and put it up in a high ponytail as R&B music plays softly in the background. It's my favorite 'do to wear, and not to mention easy to maintain. I apply some gel to my edges to get an extra sleek look, then spritz it with some olive oil hair spray for a nice shine and hold. I put on my school uniform and then look through my selection of shoes. Hmm. I think I'm in the mood to go Wakandan today. I pull out my combat boots, which I added my Melanin touch to, and I'm good to go.

"Melanin, let's go," my mom calls from downstairs. "You don't want to be late for school. I know you want to earn that award!"

"Coming!" I reply to her.

I stop to gaze at myself in the mirror. I tilt my head as I observe my features. Sometimes, I wonder if people really see me. Large eyes, the better to see you with, thick lips, the better to tell you with, and a wide nose, the better to sense you with. The morning sunlight peeking through my blinds reflects off my coils and cocoa skin. It creates a golden, diamond-like sparkle in the mirror. The glow is on point today, not bad for a Monday. I smile. "Yup, she ready!" I say to the mirror. I grab my homework and backpack, and rush downstairs.

I get to the kitchen and reach for a blueberry Nutri-Grain bar, my fav, and a K-Cup. My mom darts her eyes at me.

"Nice try, young lady, nice try," she says as she motions for me to put the cup down.

"Yes, ma'am," I say, putting the K-Cup down, somewhat disappointed. "But, come on, Mom. I've had a latte before—same thing. And you know like *all* the kids at school drink coffee. They're worse than the teachers when they don't get their morning fix."

"Well, when has it ever been justifiable to do something just because other people are doing it? If your classmates were—"

"Yes, I know," I interject. "If my classmates were to jump off a bridge, would I do so too?" I reply, as I open the fridge to grab a yogurt.

My mom smiles as she walks over to the Keurig to make herself a cup of coffee. "Actually, I was going to say, if your classmates were *my* kids, I wouldn't want them needing a fix off of anything."

"Touché," I reply with a nod.

My mom grabs two Stevia packets. "Pass me the creamer please, sweetheart."

I pass my mom the creamer and then turn to head out the door.

"Aren't you forgetting something, Melanin?" asks my mom.

I duck my head back inside the doorway. "Oh, I love you!" I reply as I give her a kiss on the cheek.

"I love you, too. But I meant your permission slip to go to the African American History museum. I left it on the fridge for you," she replies, pointing to the refrigerator door.

"Oh, man. Thanks! I thought I had already packed it in my stuff. I love you twice as much now," I say to her with a chuckle. "Oh, and don't you forget to take a break to eat your lunch today! You have to take care of yourself in order to take care of others," I remind her, putting on my adult voice.

"Awe, I swear you are an old soul, Melanin. Remind me again how you have gotten so wise."

"Some people say I take after my parents," I reply with a wink and head back out the door.

My mom helps keep me accountable, as she tells me, and she has so much knowledge. She is the director at the Smithsonian National Archive Museum and serves on the school board committee for my school as vice president.

She always has information she is sharing with me, like how hot water freezes at a faster rate than cold water when placed in the freezer—I know, mind blown!—and how I come from royal blood. Sometimes, I just smile and agree, because I don't want her to go into one of her long spiels; I would definitely be late to wherever I needed to be in that case. But all jokes aside, I honestly don't know how she does all that she does, but I'm pretty sure that she has the Wonder Woman logo underneath her shirt.

I live in Washington, DC, with my mom and dad. We live in a row house in the Navy Yard District. We're at the top of the incline, so we can see the National Baseball Stadium from our back terrace. Springtime in the Yard is amazing! The night air smells of charcoal and happiness. Even more so after our Nationals baseball team won their first World Series title. So, they are drawing in a big crowd for this new season. Go Nats!

So, I'm not actually a big sports fan, but my dad is, and I love going to games with him. He travels a lot for work, so when he's home, we make every minute count. Plus, there is nothing like the energy that fills a stadium packed with fans. I can appreciate the comradery that spreads through different types of people uniting over a common interest.

My parents met at college at a sporting event, so it holds a type of nostalgia for them. My dad was a football player for Howard University, and my mother was the manager of a rival football team. That didn't stop my dad from approaching my mom, though. He says he took his shot and it paid off. It was back in the day before people used social media like a photo album. I'm grateful for that, though, because I love flipping through their actual photo albums, and it makes me feel like I was there with them.

I'm an only child, so I'm fortunate to be able to get my parents' free time to myself. While I love our small family and how things are, it would be great to be a big sister, though. The thought of having the opportunity to help shape their life, to be a positive influence, to teach them right from wrong, to dress them up in adorable outfits, and share them on Instagram, of course...that's definitely something I get excited about.

CHAPTER 2
Shirley Chisholm Prep

I'M IN THE SEVENTH GRADE at Shirley Chisholm Preparatory Middle School, formerly known as Robert Lee Middle. I love my school! We're in the heart of DC. We sometimes have our lunches on the National Mall during the warm times of the year. Yes, you read that correctly! Our school is literally steps away from the historic Smithsonian museums, and you can see the National Monument clear as day. You just go out our school's front door, turn right to take a stroll down the street, and you're met with food trucks and history. Even when the school year is over, the school still hosts rooftop viewing parties for Juneteenth and the Fourth of July to see the fireworks. It's like having front row seats to the Superbowl, I tell ya. Okay, so maybe not that impressive, but certainly a showstopper.

We are one of the top private middle schools in Washington, DC. We're known for our science, technology, engineering, art, and math programs, which we just call STEAM. Our school has prepped and prepared some of the finest in the country, including Nobel Peace Prize recipients, Oscar winners, and several important people on the Hill—even a few in Congress! Last year, the mayoral debate was held and televised from our auditorium.

Some people think that the seventh grade is easy, or that we're still just kids, but seventh grade is the year where you supposedly leave your childish ways behind and become a young adult. We don't even get to have recess anymore. We get a "reflection break," where we go to the rooftop to meditate. Now don't get me wrong—the scenery is stunning, almost magical if I dare to be cheesy. It's just not recess, though. The running around, high-jumping, strong-kicking, energetic-leaping type of recess that gets all that pent-up energy out. I don't know who decided to have this spa escape on the rooftop of a middle school, but I most definitely believe it was one of the teachers.

We're about to enter the Week of Responsibility at our school. It's sort of a rite of passage for every seventh grader. It's made up of honesty, respect, fairness, compassion, accountability, and courage. Each day consists of a different theme that promotes awareness and discussion around the topic at hand. Each class cohort is responsible for coming up with an activity that engages the students and promotes equity around the topic. This could be done through a skit, song, event, or questionnaire. The choice is ours, as long as it meets the standards set in place. At the end of the week, the seventh-grade teachers pick one student from each cohort who has demonstrated all those qualities to be the Teacher of the Day for their cohort.

The Teacher of the Day gets to help plan the lessons for a day, and they plan and lead one lesson on their own. They get to be a part of the staff meeting and share ideas and help the homeroom teacher decide on the setup for the flex seating. A flexible seating classroom is not set up like a traditional classroom with just rows of student desks and chairs. Instead, most of that is replaced with more comfortable options, like bean bag chairs, bouncy balls, pillow seats, wobble stools, standing desks, and even a lounge area. It makes the classroom more accessible for students, as it allows for a variety of learning styles, I am told. All I know is, I'm all for it. Each Teacher of the Day also gets to decide the lunch menu for one day of the week and make morning announcements from the principal's office that day. The icing on the cake is they get an automatic A in all subjects for the day, and they are put into the running for the award of Principal of the Day, which includes the eighth grade Teacher of the Day recipients as well.

I've had my eye on that prize since I was in the fourth grade. The students used to talk about the honor that comes from receiving that award. They would hear about it from older siblings. Past Teacher of the Day recipients have gone on to do bigger and better things, like student body president, patrol captain, school board student rep, and morning announcement anchor, to name a few.

Since as long as I could remember, I wanted to be like my parents and be in a role where I feel like I can help others. They are involved in helping to make the world a better place. I know that sounds super corny, but it's true. When I think about what I want to be when I get older, there are a lot of things I can imagine myself choosing, like news anchor, investigative journalist, district attorney, House Representative, or CEO of a nonprofit. So, obviously, I don't know exactly where or what I'll end up doing, but whatever I decide to do, I know that at the end of the day, I want to feel good about myself and who I am. I want to have a positive impact on others' lives.

CHAPTER 3
Pledge of Allegiance

I GET TO SCHOOL and see Miss Miller, our homeroom and English teacher, greeting students at the door of her classroom. I settle in quickly and see my best friend, Brianna Rodriguez, aka Bri, struggling with getting her things in order. I've known Bri since I was like zero years old. Her parents are best friends with mine, so we're really like sisters. They met at a Lamaze class, where women go to practice breathing while they are pregnant. I guess it's good for the baby. Usually the woman's partner goes with her to offer support and hold her hand and stuff. As my mom tells it, once, a woman went into labor and my dad and another man freaked out and passed out at the same time. My mom and the wife of the other man both had to comfort their husbands and help them with their breathing as they came to. That Lamaze really came in handy that day. As you probably guessed, the other couple was Bri's parents. They've been best friends ever since. But both my dad and her dad deny that things went down like that, and they say that when they stood up to try to help, they slipped...at the same time...from a level floor. But hey, it could happen...I guess.

I help Bri sharpen her pencils and organize her desk, as usual. And by organize, I mean take the scattered selection of eyeshadow, collection of lip glosses, and her specialty snack mix of Takis and sour gummy worms off of her desk to make room for learning. And yes, you heard that correctly. She mixes Takis chips and sour gummy worms and calls that her spicy sour mix. I don't understand how she even eats that, but apparently, it's better than warm pie on a Sunday afternoon.

Bri grabs my homework with hers, and places it in the homework bin before catching up.

"Did you catch the new episode of *New Money* last night?" asked Bri. "Girl, it was sooo good! Terrance is my boo and Ava is everything!"

I squint my face. "Now you know my parents are not going to let me watch that show."

"Why? It's TV-14, and you're 13...sooo pretty much the same thing," laughs Bri.

"Oh, okay, I'll be sure to relay that information to my parents," I reply with a smirk.

Just then Alexander and Annabella Carnegie, aka Alex and Bella, walk up. They're twins and known as the Carnegie duo because they are each other's shadows; if you see one, the other is bound to be a second from sight. Bella is our other table partner, and Alex is not a fan of his table cluster, so he always waits until he has to sit down to make his way there.

"Ugh, sorry we're late. Alex got stuck in his uniform shirt again," Bella says, laughing.

Alex cuts his eyes at Bella. "No, I didn't! Why do you keep telling people that?!" Alex yells.

"I'm sorry. Was that not you I walked in on this morning with his arms halfway through the shirt sleeves and head struggling to see daylight?" questions Bella. "Oh, right that must have been my other twin...Casper."

Bri bursts out laughing. "She done said Casper, I can't!"

"Dude really, you're going to add to her shenanigans?" questions Alex to Bri.

Bri puts her hands up and shrugs. "Funny is funny. I don't discriminate," replies Bri.

So, Alex and Bella aren't really supposed to be in the same cohort together, but their parents insisted, saying that the separation would cause anxiety. I feel their parents might be the ones a tad bit anxious about them not being together, however. They're recently divorced, and I guess trying to keep things as normal as possible for Alex and Bella. I'd been to their house a couple of times before the divorce and they always seemed so happy, like cover-of-a-magazine happy.

Anyway, their dad is on the school board committee with my mom and is a legislative litigator—that's a fancy way of saying a lawyer for government issues. But yeah, I just think the school didn't really want to deal with the hassle, so they agreed. Plus, they actually do work well together...well, besides the occasional bickering—and that one time Bella kicked Alex in the shin for siding with Carl during an argument. But besides that, they are the yin to the other's yang.

"Y'all are too much sometimes," I say to them with a chuckle.

I finish helping Bri organize her desk as Miss Miller walks in with a student I don't recognize. "Class, this is Michael. He just transferred here from Florida. I expect everyone will help to make sure Michael feels welcome," she says.

"Yes, Miss Miller," reply some of my classmates.

Miss Miller points to an empty desk in my table cluster where Michael can sit. "Red tables, can you please help Michael get settled in?" asks Miss Miller. "And Alex, please go sit in your cluster. They won't bite."

Bri and I nod with a smile. We're kind of like the welcoming committee. We don't really have a welcoming committee, though; we kind of voluntarily took on the role because, well, someone had to do it.

Alex hesitates to move, pretending like he didn't hear Miss Miller.

"Oh, I see you took too long, so now you can sit by yourself at the gray table for the class," says Miss Miller to Alex. Alex groans as he makes his way to his new seat for the day.

Michael walks over quietly and sits down without making much eye contact with anyone. He has the stature of a basketball player. He has piercing grayish-green eyes, short curly black hair, and he's rocking Balenciagas with his uniform. We eagerly introduce ourselves to him, but he gives a faint smile without saying anything and looks back down at his desk.

"Well, lovely conversation," Bri whispers to me sarcastically. I motion for her to cut it out.

"Alright, class, it's time for the morning announcements," Miss Miller tells us.

She turns on the TV, and the Pledge of Allegiance slide comes up. When the class stands, I see that Michael does not. I see Miss Miller notices, but she doesn't say anything to him. My classmates notice, too. Some of them cut their eyes in his direction and some look confused. "Is he deaf?" whispers one student to another.

Michael doesn't move, and I mean not at all. He doesn't unpack or read or engage in anything else. He just sits in silence, glaring down at his desk like he could see through it. Real strange-like.

Once the Pledge is over, the class sits down, and a few students are still looking at Michael. He still doesn't look up. He just keeps his eyes on his see-through desk.

Carl, the resident mean kid and a fourth-generation student at our school, looks at Michael and blurts out, "I guess some people here aren't proud to be American!"

Carl's minions burst into laughter and give Carl a few high fives. Some other students chuckle. The level-headed students, like myself, just ignore him. That's usually the best way to deal with someone like Carl. Otherwise, we'd end up having another fiasco of '19. Let's just say Sam is still trying to grow back his eyebrows. Science "accident," suuurrre...

Miss Miller tells Carl to shut his face. Okay, that's not what she tells him, but she does tell him if he doesn't have anything nice to say, to not say anything at all.

Carl replies, "Yes, Miss Miller. I do apologize," as he turns around, making a face and mimicking her. Which he does often, always when he is out of eyesight. It's like he has being a jerk down to a science.

CHAPTER 4

Crudités & Macarons

THE LUNCH BELL RINGS, and you can hear the halls flood with conversation and chatter from hungry students. We have a guest chef in today, from a new restaurant that just opened near Capitol Hill, preparing two of his specialty dishes, so the lunchroom is more crowded than usual. I select the chicken Dijon with an assortment of crudités on the side and two pistachio macarons. Delectable! I see Bri and some other students from our homeroom sitting at the bay near the window and head toward them. I squeeze in at the end of the table next to Bri.

"Hey, Melanin, I was really impressed with the speech you gave for Model UN the other day," says Alex. "It sounded very professional...very Angela Rye-like."

I look up, blushing. Wow, Angela Rye is only like one of the most impressive and influential voices for equitable change in America's political process in our time. And not equitable like in real estate, but like trying to create fair standards and processes. My mom explains it like this: equity and equal are not the same thing. If everything was equal, those who are disadvantaged would still be at a loss. However, if things are equitable, situations are more fair and balanced. Like if someone can't see, they get glasses, right? But if you can see perfectly fine, why would you put the glasses on? Like, people need to stop trying to wear somebody else's glasses.

"Umm, Earth to Melanin..." says Alex.

I blink out of my daze. "Oh, wow! High praise! I could only hope to be anything like her. Thank you," I reply.

"So, what is everyone planning on doing for their service project?" asks Bella.

Bri scrunches up her face and replies, "Ugh, I don't want to think about that."

I chuckle. "That's not going to make the project magically disappear. Plus, at least we get to pick partners this year. You know the eighth graders were crying about how they had to do solo projects and it's unfair and whatnot."

Bri laughs. "No one is concerned with those eighth graders. They are always complaining about something. Oooh, side note, did you hear how Bobby P. broke into a flood of tears when Melissa broke up with him at the Spring Fling Dance?! The poor dude was left standing alone in the middle of the dance floor with tears rolling down his face while people did the Toosie Slide around him. Like sir, please leave the dance floor."

"You're not right Bri," says Alex shaking his head. "Guys have feelings too!"

"What I dooo?" snickers Bri faking confused. "I mean, like that would have been in his best interest to get some privacy in that moment."

Bella interjects, "Forget about eighth grade drama. What about seventh grade? Oh my gosh, I felt soooo embarrassed for that new kid today."

"Shoot, I'm happy I wasn't him," Bri says, nodding. "And he just sat there and took everything Carl had to say."

"Maybe because he knows he's wrong for not standing up for the Pledge. So, what would he say?" Alex points out as he grabs one of my macarons.

I grab the macaron out of Alex's hand quickly before he has a chance to bite it. "His name is Michael," I say.

"Oh, we seem to have triggered a nerve," jokes Bella.

I cut my eyes at her. People are always trying to make something out of nothing.

"It's not even that. I'm just tired of Carl treating people so badly and getting away with it. It's so sixth grade. We're really too old to still have students acting so immature."

"I was just joking. And I know Carl is the worst," Bella quickly says.

"Yes, we *all* know Carl is the worst. Even the teachers. I've definitely seen some veins pop out of their neck while dealing with him," laughs Bri. "Buuut Michael is quite cute, wouldn't you say? Hmmm, Melanin and Michael has a nice ring to it, don't you think?" says Bri as she nudges me on the shoulder.

I roll my eyes and continue eating my lunch.

"No, no, I wouldn't say that. Melanin requires someone cool and confident. Not scared and feeble," replies Alex.

"Who, someone like...yooou?" jokes Bella, pointing both of her index fingers at Alex.

I take a deep breath. "Wow, y'all are exhausting. Can I enjoy my macarons in peace?" I ask them.

"Hm, speaking of the devil," says Bri.

I look up and see Carl and his friends making their way into the cafeteria. They bypass the other students in line to get their food. You hear students mumbling with annoyance. Carl and his friends walk out of line with enough food to feed a whole football team. They always sit on the platform area in the cafeteria and claims it as theirs, so to avoid drama, no one else dares to sit there. Carl walks toward their seats, but then catches a glimpse of Michael sitting near the water fountain and reroutes toward him. Oh gosh, this is not going to be good.

Carl and his friends reach the table where Michael is sitting. "Hey, bro, we are going to need these seats," Carl says to Michael as he pushes Michael's tray away from him.

Michael looks up at Carl with a snarl as he jumps up and hits the table with his fist. The two boys stand face to face. They are so close their noses are almost touching.

Silence falls upon the cafeteria. Michael clenches his jaw so tightly, what seems like a hundred veins pops out of his neck. Michael then takes a deep breath and replies, "I'm already done, it's all yours...bro," as he taps the table and walks off.

"Ooooop, that new kid just punked him," whispers a student.

Carl's cheeks turn rosy. Carl's friends remain quiet.

"Come on, let's go to our table. This one looks dirty," says Carl to his friends as he walks off in the other direction.

CHAPTER 5
Once Upon a Time

FOR THE NEXT COUPLE OF DAYS, Carl and his minions take pleasure in finding issue with anything and everything Michael does, and they make sure that everyone knows it. He'll wait until there isn't a teacher around or they're too busy with teacher stuff to bother him. Have you ever seen how a hyena sizes up their prey? Well, yeah, imagine that. Now, I'm not calling anyone a hyena, but I mean...if the laugh fits. Anyway, Michael could just cough, and Carl will yell, "Ronaaaaa virus!"

Bullying is nothing new for Carl. One time, Carl and his crew kept making fun of a kid named Billy about his hairline. Carl told him it was shaped like the McDonald's arch and starting singing "Bah-da-bum-bah-bah, I'm lovin' it!" as he threw fries at him. Now come on, premeditated much?

I could see Billy trying to hide his emotions, but he's a sensitive kid and couldn't keep the floodgates from opening. Billy cried so hard he hyperventilated, then threw up and passed out. He was out for only for a few seconds, but still. A group of students and I rushed to get help. By the time a teacher got over there, Billy had come to and propped himself up against the playground slide, still hyperventilating a bit. After the teacher made sure Billy was okay, Carl was asked to sit out for the rest of recess. His friends just sat with him and played on their Nintendo Switches... which they are not supposed to have. Later, Carl was heard bragging about how the principal called his parents, and his parents had to set him straight. Looks like he surely learned his lesson.

Carl likes to have an audience before he attacks his prey. He'll look around to see who's watching and gets louder and louder to draw people in, but he is careful to make sure it's not an adult. The next day, Billy came back to school with a fresh new haircut. Carl asked him if he had to sell his gear to pay for it because his clothes looked like trash. Yup, Carl...he's lovely...

Surprisingly, Carl and I used to be friends. His mom and my mom both went to college together and pledged the same sorority. After college they were roommates for a while before my dad proposed to my mom and they moved in together. My mom ended up getting pregnant four months before Carl's mom. So, our families were pretty close. There is actually a picture of us taking a bath together when we were like a year old. I could never understand why parents do stuff like that, though. I know they think it's the cutest thing ever, but they do know we are going to get older one day and see this stuff, right?!

Our friendship ended in the fifth grade when I discovered that an alien had inhabited Carl's body. He changed that year; he was no longer the Carl that would have sleepovers with me and Bri. Apparently, one day a group of boys were making fun of Carl when they found out he attended my spa birthday party and wore a face mask. They were calling him names and saying he was a fairy boy. Carl responded by telling them that he only went to my party because I had kissed him and begged him to go, and I promised to do his homework for a week. What the what?!

All of a sudden, he was Cool Carl and acting brand new. When I heard the rumors, I was livid, like mad, really mad. I tried to give him the benefit of the doubt, but when I went to talk to him, he got all defensive and asked me why I was sweating him. Boy had gotten me all the way twisted! What's worse, he waited until I got to the cafeteria for lunch to really show off, where all his *boys* would be present to witness the foolery. He had the audacity to approach me and say he couldn't handle me "smothering him" and was breaking up with me.

Now I don't recall everything that took place after that, but I do remember feeling hot all over and yelling at him, asking how he can break up with someone that he never dated. He responded for me to not make a scene or lie and that I just needed to accept the fact that it was over.

Yup, it was over, alright...ten years of friendship, just like that. How could someone who had been my friend for all those years just turn on me like that? And I had done nothing wrong to him. I did feel our friendship drifting apart prior to our fallout, though. We started liking different stuff, wanted to hang out with different people, and spent our time engaged in different things. Never in a million years, though, would I have thought he'd go from friend to foe.

I was so hurt and mad in that moment that I became someone I didn't recognize. I knocked Carl's food tray on the floor and then dumped my yogurt parfait on his head as I dared him to tell another lie.

I got sent to the principal's office and had to attend detention for the first time ever in my life. They told my parents that since it was my first time getting in trouble, it wouldn't be noted on my record, but the shame stayed with me.

My mom and his mom tried to talk about it, but they ended up getting into a disagreement and haven't talked much since then, which I also feel bad about because obviously I'm part of the reason why my mom's longtime friendship ended. My mom says it wasn't my fault and there were already other rooted issues, but I know I didn't help the situation. I told myself from that moment on, I would never let someone else's actions negatively dictate mine.

CHAPTER 6

The Assembly

WE HAVE A RIBBON cutting assembly today to honor the Charles' for their monetary donation to fund the construction of our east wing, which will house Chisholm's new state-of-the-art aquatic and recreational center. In honor of the Charles' generous donation, the facility will be named after them.

Bri and I leave fifth period and make our way to the auditorium. We get there and see two generations of the Charles' sitting on the stage in royal fashion. Dr. Campbell, our school's principal, walks onto the stage. The chatter from the audience of students comes to a halt. He goes through his spiel of thanking the Charles' for their generosity and the impact they are having on young lives. Our school band plays a song in honor of them, and then Mr.

Charles III takes the giant scissors and cuts the ribbon, symbolizing the grand opening of the Charles' Aquatic and Rec Center.

After the assembly is over, I stay behind to help stack the chairs from the stage and clean up with a few students. I look up and see Dr. Campbell approach Mr. Charles III and his wife.

"Thank you so much for being here today, and for your family's continued efforts to help support our school and students," Dr. Campbell starts. "I reached out by phone a couple of times in the past few weeks to speak with you about your son, Carl, and what some of the other students are reporting about his behavior toward them. Your assistant told me that she'd relay the message for you to call me back. I understand you both are very busy, so I thought it might be best to just speak with you in person since you're already here. Do you both have a few minutes to spare to meet with me in my office?" asked Dr. Campbell.

"Yes, I received those messages. I meant to get back to you, but you know how difficult it can be to get a free moment in a busy schedule when you're the boss. Everyone needs your time! And coffee is not going to make itself. Well...neither do I, but I sign off on the checks," chuckles Mr. Charles.

Mrs. Charles interjects, "You know middle school is a very trying time for kids. They are too old to be young and too young to be old. They are becoming young adults and trying to find themselves, and that can be a very scary and fragile time for them. So, it's expected that sometimes they will act out a bit or be a little silly...that's not unheard of. But we also know that this school does an amazing job with helping to guide its students during this difficult time. And at the end of the day, kids will be kids, right? What can you do about that?"

Mr. Charles adds, "And I would know, since my siblings and I went to this school, and our father before that, and so on. So, our family has a long history with this...establishment. One we value and take much pride in, which is why we continue to financially support this school. And I would hate for that relationship to have to change over a little innocent schoolyard fun. The school's focus should be on a quality education—not entertaining childish rumors," states Mr. Charles.

Dr. Campbell sighs and takes off his glasses. "Yes, we would hate for the relationship to change as well. And that certainly is not my intent. I just want to make sure the school environment is habitable for all students."

"Well, we are all on the same page then. Great talk! I'll have to pencil you in for coffee sometime. Just make an appointment with my assistant." Mr. Charles disingenuously smiles. "Well, we have to run. I've already been out of the office for half a day to come here, so I need to make sure my coffeehouses are still up and running."

The Charles' begin to leave and see Carl goofing off by the entrance of the auditorium, dropping marbles down the walkway. Mr. Charles cuts his eyes at Carl and signals for him to come over to him. His friends see this and disperse quickly out the doors. Carl walks over to them reluctantly, with his head draped low. "Hey, Dad..." Carl musters up.

Before he could get another word out, Mr. Charles jerks him up by the shoulder.

"What did I tell you about embarrassing us in public!" exclaims Mr. Charles. Carl looks terrified. "I have no idea where you learned this behavior. This is ridiculous! Best believe you'll be taking the metro home today, young man. If you can't behave properly, then don't expect us to be seen with you," scolds Mr. Charles as he shakes his head. "No one has time for your antics, Carl. Keep it up, and you'll be at home during spring break—alone—while the rest of the family goes on vacation. And just like the past summer, I will not lose any sleep about leaving you behind. If you want to act in this manner, then I'll treat you accordingly."

I can hear Carl sniffling to fight back tears.

"Honey, he's just a child. He doesn't mean any harm," replies Mrs. Charles.

"Let's go, Patricia!" says Carl's dad strongly.

Mrs. Charles looks at Carl sympathetically and gives him a quick kiss on the forehead before she follows her husband out the door.

Carl turns and sees me looking in his direction, his eyes puffy and cheeks beet-red. I look away quickly, trying to pretend like I didn't see anything.

At the end of the day, I see Carl by his locker. I begin to walk by him, but something makes me stop to talk to him.

"Hey, um...I just wanted to let you know that I think your dad just wants to see you live up to your potential," I say.

"Thanks for your input, Melanin, but I don't really care what you think. And if this is your way of trying to get an invite to my spring bash soirée, you can forget about it. Desperation is not a good look on you," replies Carl.

I give out a deep sigh. I should have known better. Why did I even bother? *Choke on your tongue, Carl!* I picture myself saying to him. Instead I reply, "Okay, Carl...you have a great day! Don't let that ego trip you up."

I walk away thinking, *He can go kick rocks with flip-flops!*

CHAPTER 7

_____ is *Beautiful*

THE HOMEROOM BELL RINGS to dismiss students to their first period class. Dr. Campbell comes on the loudspeaker. "Seventh graders, please report to the front lobby. Seventh graders, please report to the front lobby."

Today is our day of fairness and compassion. The seventh-grade class voted on a museum to visit that would align with reflection around our theme of the day. There were so many good choices that it was hard to pick just one, but the African American History Museum had the most votes. I am beyond excited! And it's lucky for us that we are so close to the museums. We will have a chance to visit other museums later, also.

I mentally check off the essentials to take with me. Cell phone for Instagrammable photos—check. Okay, good to go! I'm joking! I, of course, have my money, some backup travel size hair pomade, and Fenti lip illuminator (lip gloss, to those not hip) in my pack...aka, fanny pack for the originators. But these are *très* stylish—not your mom's fanny packs.

Miss Miller gives us our itinerary and breaks us into groups so that we know which chaperone to check in with. Bri walks up to me. "Hey girl, hey! I see we've been grouped together. Ayyye! Buuuut along with us is Carl and a few of his clones. Booo. This is gonna be super fun!" mocks Bri, as she fakes a smile and rolls her eyes.

I chuckle. "Well, I'm not letting anyone ruin this day for me.

"True," agrees Bri as we head out the lobby doors.

"Okay, students, please remember to carry yourselves as upstanding citizens of Shirley Chisholm Prep and make sure you represent us well," Miss Miller announces as we're heading out the door. "We will meet at the cafe at twelve o'clock sharp for lunch. Don't be late," she reminds us.

I see Carl and his boys already outside throwing water balloons at passing cars. Miss Miller spots them.

"Excuse me!" Miss Miller exclaims as she heads toward them with urgency. "You have got to be kidding me! Don't think I won't have you all stay back if you can't conduct yourselves like young men!" Miss Miller spurs as she puts her hand out for them to give her the balloons.

The group of boys reluctantly give them to her as they grunt and complain.

"Please let this be the only time I need to address you in this way today, scholars," Miss Miller informs with a stern tone, as she tosses the balloons into the trash.

Carl acts offended. "Well, I have neva!" he replies, with his left hand clutching his chest.

Miss Miller stares at Carl without blinking. "And I'm sure that's the problem, Carl. I'm sure that's the problem," she replies, shaking her head. She motions for them to walk, and they begin walking unenthused.

"Bro, why are we walking, though? The school really couldn't get us transportation?" Carl complains to his boys. "I mean, I could have easily taken an Uber. Like, these are limited edition kicks," I overhear Carl saying to his friends as he points to his shoes.

Just then, Michael walks by, which catches Carl's attention. "Whew, what's that smell?" Carl yells out as he waves his hand in front of his nose. "Oh, my bad, y'all, it's just Michael," Carl jokes. Carl and his friends burst out laughing. You would have thought they had front row seats to a Kevin Hart show.

Michael pays them no mind and just keeps walking. I'm pretty sure I was more annoyed by them than he was. Hmm. He must do yoga or something.

I swear it's like Carl complains just so people can hear his voice. I hate it. I speed up my pace to get some distance from him.

"Dang, I didn't know you were trying to run a marathon today, Melanin!" says Bri as she jogs to catch up with me. "The museum is not going anywhere."

I smirk at her and slow down a bit. "No one told you to wear heels today. Not to mention, the flyer definitely said to wear sensible shoes," I reply, pointing at her feet.

Bri looks at me and gasps. "First, these are not heels. They are wedges! Second, these are sensibly cute. Thank you very much."

"And ya feet is gonna be sensibly hurting by the end of the day," I say. We both laugh.

As we get closer to the National Monument, I see the light reflecting off the bronze exterior panels of the African American History Museum. The design is so beautiful and unique. It's not like any other museum on the Mall.

We enter the museum and are greeted by an energetic tour guide. "Good morning, and welcome to the African American History Museum! My name is Mr. Q, and I will be your docent for today. What is a docent, you ask? Well, we're just like tour guides. And that's what I will be doing today, guiding you through parts of the museum. After that you will have a chance to break up into groups to view the rest of the museum on your own."

Carl raises his hand. "Yes, young man in the back, what is your question?" asks Mr. Q.

"Do you mean to tell me that we all have to stay together for this? It's like fifty of us. Miss Miller, what's up with that?! Why in the world did you even group us up then?"

Carl asks as he shakes his head. "Doesn't make any sense if you ask me," he continues.

Miss Miller turns to face Carl with a creepy-looking smile on her face. I can tell she's less than pleased with him. "That's one young man," she whispers to him. "Please don't make me have to call your dad today." Carl quickly quiets up.

She's talking about strikes. Everyone gets three a day and after that, *you're oooouuut!* Okay, well, you don't actually get put out or anything like that, but you do get some type of consequence.

Miss Miller turns back to face the docent. "I apologize for the interruption, Mr. Q. Please go on."

Mr. Q nods and continues. "Are y'all ready to experience the history of the richness and diversity of the African American experience in America?!" Mr. Q asks us excitedly. There are scattered cheers and applause.

This is like my third time here, and I still have not made my way through all the sections thoroughly yet. My mom was able to get us tickets for the opening day a couple years back, so I had the privilege of being one of the first viewers to experience the museum. But I was just a young kid in elementary school. I didn't really get the significance of it then.

"Now, please keep in mind that there is some sensitive material inside the galleries," our docent warns us. "A red border is around those images in the exhibit to warn you of the type of content. If at any time you get overwhelmed by any of the sights, we do have counselors on site to help assist you with how you are feeling," Mr. Q continues. The class nods.

Carl turns and whispers to his friends, "Yeah, for the crybabies." They chuckle amongst themselves. Carl looks back and sees Miss Miller staring a hole into the side of his head, and then quickly turns back around to face Mr. Q.

"You will see pain and suffering today, but you'll also see strength, resilience, and triumph," Mr. Q says proudly. "Okay, let's get this show on the road!" Mr. Q says with a clap.

Mr. Q begins our curated tour, which means he's giving us detailed information about the things we are seeing. He starts us in the History Galleries. We all get into a giant glass elevator. Everyone looks so intrigued. Some class-mates began taking selfies already, and Bella starts to record on her iPhone. "Hey followers, just checking in. I am about to experience the past, a trip through American history. I will be sure to keep y'all updated on my journey and my reactions to it. I'll be checking back in with you laters. Much love. Bella," she says as she blows a kiss at her phone screen.

"Girl you are doing the most, calm down," says Bri to Bella.

Bella looks over at Bri unamused. "Now, I'm going to have to edit you out. Thanks," Bella replies back to Bri.

As we ride down in the elevator, I see a timeline on a black wall, and I realize we are going back in time. The elevator stops, and the timeline reads *1400s*.

Mr. Q guides us through the Slavery and Freedom floor. He talks about the violent capture of Africans in their country and being forced to become slaves. Some classmates look upset and others are not really paying attention, a few on their phones texting or playing games. I spot Michael. He's been rather quiet, not saying much, but I guess that's his normal. He is intently reading the different informational plaques.

That's insane to think about, though. Imagine you're just, like, living your life, and then someone comes by and kidnaps you, says they own you now, and you have no rights or freedoms and must work for free.

Alex and some of the other boys talk about what they would have done to the capturers if they were alive back during that time.

"The testosterone is running mighty high today I see," I comment to Bri and Bella.

"The worst part is they don't even realize they are being super insensitive about the topic," says Bri as she shakes her head.

"Alex is so embarrassing sometimes," sighs Bella.

"I mean, you were just recording for the masses like point two seconds ago. So, yea..." Bri says to Bella.

"Umm, excuse me?" questions Bella.

"Girl, I said what I said," responds Bri.

"Well, my apologies for wanting others to experience this rich, cultural experience with me," replies Bella as she flips her hair and continues walking.

"Okay, ladies, let's show a bit of *compassion* toward each other," I say, trying to ease the tension.

Bri laughs. "What? She knows I am just playing with her."

"Okay, it's time for us to continue our journey in time to the era of segregation," announces Mr. Q.

The students quickly gather to go up the ramp, a couple pushing to get in front of others.

I stop at an exhibit that displays two people whose names I haven't heard of before. Clara Brown and Robert Smalls. Brown was a pioneer who saved her money and pretty much invested in real estate and gave back to her community. And Smalls was a slave who escaped and helped others escape to freedom during the Civil War by commandeering a Confederate ship. He later became a US Congressman. As I'm reading through their information, I feel someone standing behind me. I turn around, and it's Michael.

"Wow, pretty inspiring for that day and age," he says while still looking at the display.

I smile and respond, "Yeah, it really is."

We both stand there, almost studying the exhibit. Meanwhile, students are going crazy with their snaps and selfies. They look like paparazzi during a Beyoncé sighting.

Mr. Q then guides us to the next part of our tour. He tells us that this area is a bit more sensitive and that anyone who may not want to view it may step to the side or sit in the theatre to watch a quick video about the fight for freedom. A few students decide to stay back, and a chaperone waits with them.

We learn about the brave people, both black and white, who risked their lives so that we could have a better life; their courage to speak up and risk their safety helped shape society for us today. Like Emmett Till's mom for sharing the tragic and horrifying story of what happened to her teenage son.

As I'm listening to the information Mr. Q is telling us, I get a big lump in my throat; it's hard to hear some of this information because it's so unimaginable, so inhumane. Everyone is listening intently, and a few classmates even tear up. To my pleasant surprise, even Carl is engaged in what Mr. Q is saying at this point.

"Man, that's messed up," comments Carl. He sniffles and a tear rolls down his cheek. I stand there in utter shock, and for a split second it seems like Carl and I are in the same universe. He looks up and sees me looking at him. I give him a little smile and nod. He quickly wipes the tear away from his face and turns the other way, pushing a classmate out of his way, telling them to "watch out."

We are then led up the ramp to see the gallery called A Changing America.

Ahh, there is so much to see, I get giddy just thinking about it. In particular, the Women in Power exhibits. As the tour continues, I feel my stomach tighten. With each passing minute, I get more and more anxious to go visit that exhibit. It's one of my favorites in the museum. I aspire to be just a fraction as amazing and inspiring as some of those women have been.

I get to the top of the ramp and turn the corner to enter the gallery and am greeted with the raised fists of the Black Panther women. Chills travel down my spine. But not in an *Oh my gosh, I'm scared* way, but in an *Oh my gosh, this is amazing* way. Unapologetically black and female—I'm in awe of that image.

I see the Black Feminism section to the side and head to it without waiting for the group. I've been waiting all day to get here. One of the first women I see listed is Angela Davis, who was a college professor and an intellectual leader and symbol of the Black Power movement. The exhibit talks about how black feminists attempted to empower all women regardless of their race. They spoke out against all forms of oppression and fought to bring about social change. I smile as I wonder if I would have been that brave to speak up.

I look up and make eye contact with Miss Miller. She smiles and then motions for me to come back to the group. I head back over, slipping in behind Bri.

Mr. Q stops in front of the Black Power movement section and explains the reasoning behind the movement. "The purpose of the Black Power movement was to try to combat the racial oppression by demonstrating self-respect and racial pride, as well as celebrating the cultural accomplishments of black people around the world. Can someone tell me a current movement that this might remind you of?" asks Mr. Q to the group.

Alex's hand is the first to raise. "Yes, to the eager hand right there," Mr. Q says as he points to Alex.

"It's reminiscent of the Black Lives Matter movement," answers Alex proudly.

"Yes, very good. That is correct," confirms Mr. Q.

I think about our theme of the day, fairness and compassion, and I wonder how I can do a better job with this. At the end of the day, if we are trying to make a better world for all, don't we have to, like, try to be better ourselves? Maybe actually listen to one another...be kind to one another...care about one another...just a wild suggestion. Treat people the way you want to be treated is something I learned in, like, kindergarten. Hmm. Maybe a lot of people skipped kindergarten.

When we pass the Black Electoral Politics section, the students get excited to see Shirley Chisholm's name. Mr. Q spends a little extra time talking about her impact since our school is named for her. Mr. Q asks us what we know about Mrs. Chisholm.

A student replies, "Mrs. Chisholm was a New York Congresswoman who drew national attention by running for president in 1972."

Carl starts to laugh. "Well, thank you very much, Sherlock, for reading *verbatim* what is written down on the platform!"

The student looks embarrassed and puts her head down. Well, I see Carl's deep, reflective state didn't last for long. Miss Miller walks over to Carl. "That's two," she tells him. Carl rolls his eyes. "I didn't even do anything!" he replies with a raised voice.

"Don't make it three, Carl," she replies back. He sucks his teeth and turns back around to face Mr. Q.

We, of course, talk about Dr. Martin Luther King, Jr. and his pivotal role in the Civil Rights movement, as well as former President Barack Obama's historical feat of becoming the first black president. Talk about changing America and having it come around full circle.

Mr. Q also mentions Michelle Obama and some fun facts about Oprah Winfrey's rise to fame. Carl interrupts Mr. Q, shouting out to passing visitors, "You get a car, and you get a car, and you get a car!" Most classmates laugh.

I see Miss Miller giving Carl the teacher stare from across the room. She puts up three fingers and motions for him to come stand next to her.

"Are you serious? Always picking on me!" Carl mutters to himself as he painfully walks toward her.

Mr. Q leads us to the next ramp and has our group step to the side so others can pass us. "As I hope you all have learned today, African Americans have significantly influenced global history and culture," says Mr. Q. He wraps up his tour, ending by saying, "Just as Civil Rights and the Black Power movements pursued goals of justice and equality in the twentieth century, Americans must decide how to advance these goals into the twenty-first century. I hope this is something that each and every one of you is thinking about. How are you going to make a positive impact?" he asks. Mr. Q then thanks us for our time.

Miss Miller then dismisses us to explore the rest of the museum on our own.

One of my other favorite places in the African American History Museum is the Culture Galleries. I decide to make my way there.

I see Miss Miller standing by the reactions video with a group of students discussing how they felt about what they saw today. I approach her and tap her on the arm. "Miss Miller, is it okay if I go look at a different part of the museum?" I ask.

Miss Miller turns around with a kind smile. "Yes, no problem. Please just make sure you keep your phone close by and look out for my texts," she replies.

I eagerly nod okay. I turn to find Bri. "Hey, I'm going to go to another section. I'll be back in a little," I tell her.

"Okay, do you want me to come with?" Bri asks me.

"No, I'm okay. I kinda want to go by myself, anyway."

"'Kay, cool. Just text me when you wanna meet up. Especially before lunch so we can get good seats. And I am not sitting at the table with Carl," replies Bri. "I will eat standing up first."

"I got you," I reply with a wink and head towards the Culture Galleries.

As soon as I get there, I head to the Visual Art section which depicts various modes of American art from African American artists. The images are so beautiful, like surreal but real at the same. I mean, I know that makes no sense, but that's how I feel.

I walk through the curved walkway of the visual art exhibit, admiring the artworks from all types of African Americans. The artwork tells stories of love and self-worth, activism and freedom, and dignity and pride. It's cool to see so many different types of artwork from people who look like me. As I explore the trail of carefully placed pieces, I begin to feel warm inside, almost toasty. And not like a burning sensation, but one of comfort. I think about all that I've seen today at the museum, so many things that are uncomfortable, and just horrible. However, amid all that was wrong, triumph did ring true. It would be so easy to be bitter and cynical in a world still trying to heal itself, but just like these vivid images depict a type of hopefulness, I too am filled with hope.

I find myself standing in front of one painting, called *Arty*, and for some reason, it stops me. It is an image of a young black woman. I've seen this image before, but this time it looks different—it feels different, like it has changed.

As I stare at the portrait, taking in all the shapes and the vivid colors, an emotional wave hits me. I've never quite had this feeling before. I stand frozen, staring at the painting, feeling...I don't know, like a bit nervous and almost scared. I take a deep breath and let whatever I'm feeling sweep through me. Almost embracing it, I guess. A tear swells up in my left eye and slowly rolls down my cheek. I immediately feel a bit relieved. I feel...proud...proud to be me...proud to be black...because black is beautiful.

CHAPTER 8

Anti-Bullying

IT'S NOW THE DAY before Miss Miller picks the Teacher of the Day. Today's theme combined accountability and courage, and ironically, the focus is on anti-bullying. Each class cohort needs to come up with an activity that will promote awareness and meaningful discussion around the topic. My group decided that students will complete a bullying questionnaire where they will choose a response to who they believe they are. They will pick which role they often see themselves in—a bully, a victim, or a bystander. If they pick bully, they will need to reflect on why they are considered a bully. If they choose victim, they will reflect on strategies for how they can overcome being bullied. And if they choose bystander, they will reflect on what they can do the next time they see someone being bullied. However, the class is too busy being divided over talks of patriotism to be worried about that.

I get to our reflection break and see Carl playing basketball with his friends. He complained to his dad about not having a court, and next thing you know, the serene rooftop has a basketball court added to it. A netted makeshift wall surrounds them to prevent overthrown balls. Yes, that has happened before, hence the makeshift wall. Imagine one of the thousands of businesspeople out to grab their lunch as a basketball drops from the sky like a meteor, desecrating any food in hand. It only took one Congressman's attire stained with chicken soup, which his soul was not fond of, and we got fenced in on our rooftop getaway. Welp, what can I say...understandable.

Carl scores a three-pointer on his opponent. "Shout goes out to NIKE, checks all over me," Carl raps, imitating Drake's voice with his hands still in the air from the shot.

Michael walks out and stops to watch the game from the sidelines. Carl sees him and stops mid-shoot. "No, no, no," he chuckles, placing the basketball under his arm. "Now I *know* we don't have a spy sneaking in on our territory. As a matter of fact, since we are on US soil, the un-American people should not be allowed to even get a break," Carl announces to the group, looking at Michael.

Michael begins to walk away, but then he stops and turns around to approach Carl. Carl's friends quickly rush to his side.

"Dude, what's your problem?!" Michael says to Carl.

At this moment, it seems like the whole grade stops what they are doing to watch this exchange between Carl and Michael.

"Oh, it's looking like someone is feeling bold today!" Carl jokes. "But I suggest you keep moving if you know what's good for you, bro."

Michael rolls his eyes and turns back around to walk away.

Carl acts like he is entitled to try to tell somebody what an American is or should be. The audacity! A few of us try to shut Carl up, but he does as he pleases.

"Nobody finds you amusing Carl," I say to him.

"You're always doing too much, for what?" Bri says to him.

"Oh my, here come my fans. Always watching me, I see," replies Carl as he winks as us.

"Hey Mel, how ya doing sweetheart?"

"Don't do that."

"What's the matter? Everyone else with longer names have shortened nicknames and they are fine with it."

"Yes, because that is what they want, so that is fine. However, my name has significant meaning. My parents chose it to represent pride in the black race and for me to always remember who I am and to be proud of that. So, no, I don't want it to be shortened. I want it said in full. Melanin, not Mel...please and thank you."

"Wow, you always have to be so different, huh?"

"Just because someone is different, doesn't mean it's a bad thing. Our differences are what make us unique, and we all have them."

"Yea, yea. Thanks for that breakdown Mel, oh excuse me, I mean ME-LAN-IN."

I try to not let Carl bother me, but he knows how to get underneath my skin. It's like that's his superpower.

"Anyway, I'm sorry ladies, I can't spare any more time for you today. I already have plans with Melanin's mom and she's been pressing me about it...can't leave the lady hanging," chuckles Carl.

"Oooooo, got em!" yells out one of Carl's friends as they explode in laughter.

I stand there staring at him as I tense up. I feel that same burning sensation running through my veins that I felt back in fifth grade when he showed out that time. But this time it's different, because I'm so mad that my ears and teeth go numb. Now, I don't know what that means, but I do know he just started a problem. Hmm. Well, it looks like today is the day I fight a boy.

I jerk to approach him and Bri catches my arm, shaking her head. "Ugh, come on girl, he's not worth the energy," she says to me as she tugs my arm to walk away.

I stand there for a second, not taking my eyes off Carl. I then think about the promise I made myself last time. I take a deep breath and reply, "True, he's not worth my time," as I compose myself and walk off. I'm fortunate to have such a good friend like Bri. Letting Carl suck me into his foolishness, again, would have definitely been something I regretted.

I overhear the teacher telling Carl to cut it out, but of course that little "warning" did nothing. You'd think Carl would get tired of targeting Michael, but it's almost like he becomes more energized and determined to break him down. I wonder why. Did they meet in another lifetime and Michael stole his girl or something? But then I remember, Carl is Carl and is allowed to be Carl, so why would he stop?

During lunch, Carl's reign of terror continues. He spots Michael and makes a beeline toward him. Michael looks up and sees Carl and his friends approaching and lets out a deep breath. Carl gets to Michael's table and stops directly in front of him. "Awe, all by yourself huh?" mocks Carl. "No new friends, no new friends, no no nooo," Carl rap sings, chuckling with his boys. He then places both hands on the table and leans over Michael's lunch. "Michael, buddy, pal, you should probably go eat somewhere else where you'd feel more comfortable, like outside the borders of the US," says Carl. Some kids laugh, but some, like me, don't find it funny at all.

This is hard to watch. I feel a sinking feeling in the pit of my stomach. It's like Carl is talking to me; I feel like the fifth-grade incident is happening all over again. The crazy part of this is that I have mixed feelings about the situation, and I don't know what to make of it. I want to say something—to yell and scream at him—but my body just doesn't move. Instead, I just sit there like everyone else, uncomfortably watching, wanting to say something, but unable to. Ugh, what's wrong with me?

Michael stands up, walks around the table, and stands face-to-face with Carl. Mmm, this feels like déjà vu. Their faces are so close, they have to be feeling each other's breath. It looks like Michael has had enough. He looks like he is inwardly seething. Michael stares at Carl intensely as he clenches his fists. His eyes look dilated like a cat before it attacks. An eerie silence falls across the cafeteria. It's so quiet you could hear a pin drop. All eyes are on them. Yup, this is it. Carl is about to get wrecked. Oh no, watch Michael get all the blame, though.

Carl looks a bit uneasy and takes a step back. Michael pauses for a second then grabs his tray and walks off. Carl's friends hype him up. "Yeah, you showed him!"

Wow, I've heard of the saying "kill someone with kindness," but I didn't know people actually practiced that. But if so, that strategy is definitely *not* working with Carl.

I feel bad for Michael. I just wish Carl would leave him alone and find something positive to focus his energy on. It's obvious that what Carl says bothers Michael, so I wonder why he doesn't stand up for himself.

CHAPTER 9

Dad Knows Best

I GET HOME FROM SCHOOL and see my dad in the kitchen, making his famous roadhouse chili for dinner. The smell of my favorite meal typically fills my heart with joy, but I'm not feeling very jovial. I place my backpack in the foyer and make my way to the kitchen. My dad has the whole spread laid out. He's behind the counter chopping away at onions and peppers, singing along to music as it plays in the background.

"Your mom has a program at the museum tonight, so she'll be home later than usual," he tells me.

I climb onto a stool and place my head into the palm of my hands with my elbows resting on the table. I let out a deep sigh.

"Okay," I reply.

My dad stops cutting the vegetables and turns his head to look at me.

"Uh oh, what's wrong, baby girl? Why do you look so sad?" my dad asks, concerned.

I knew it'd be hard for me to hide my feelings from my dad. I swear he can read minds.

"Some kids from school have been picking on the new student because he doesn't stand for the Pledge of Allegiance," I tell him. "They were saying he wasn't patriotic and an enemy of the state. They said if he wasn't proud to be an American, then he needed to leave this country."

"I see. So, what did you do?"

"Well...I mean, I guess I didn't really do anything..."

"Hmm..." my dad sighs.

"I mean...I was also a bit bothered that he didn't stand for the Pledge, but I don't like that they are bullying him for it. I feel really bad for him. Now they are just picking on him about everything," I reveal to my dad.

"Why were you bothered that he didn't stand for the Pledge?" my dad asks.

"Dad, you're a soldier!" I say, as I stand up and point to the American flag we have resting above our mantel next to his uniform hat that reads *Sergeant*. "You risk your life to protect and serve this country, and you always tell me I should be a proud American."

"Honey, do you know why I became a soldier?" my dad asks as he comes from behind the counter and places his hand on my shoulder. "I'm a soldier because, yes, I am a proud American and proud to serve my country. I love America, even though America has not always loved me. It's also because I believe in the principles in which this country stands for, even when those rights were not always fairly received by all. Among those principles is the First Amendment right, freedom of speech, which means your classmate has the right to choose whether or not he participates in the Pledge. Someone exercising their First Amendment right is the definition of patriotic, in my mind, as long as they are doing so peacefully. I protect and serve America to defend our rights and liberties; I fight for those freedoms. The only thing you should ask of anyone is to be respectful, whichever choice they choose."

My dad pauses for a moment before he continues. "Melanin, you are privileged to be able to attend that school but don't forget who you are, sweetheart. Do you even know why he doesn't stand?" he asks.

"No," I reply, embarrassed. I think about how I, too, judged Michael without having insight. I feel a bit ashamed. I know I definitely wouldn't want someone doing that to me.

My dad walks back over to the chopped veggies and adds them to the pot of chili.

"Well, don't you think you should at least try to find out why before you start to judge him?" asks my dad as he looks up from stirring.

"Yeah...that's a good point," I say, smiling.

My dad always knows just what to do. I'm so grateful that I can talk to him about anything.

"Well I'm sure you'll decide the right thing to do," my dad tells me with a wink as he turns off the stove burner. "Set the table for me please, pumpkin."

I smile at my dad. "Aye, captain, my captain," I respond, saluting him. He chuckles. "How old are you again?" he jokes, saluting me back.

I pull out the plates and silverware and start setting them on the table. I think about everything that's been happening at school, not just with Michael, but the overall environment. Our school prides itself on diversity and inclusion but the actions of some students have not measured up to that standard, which is disappointing. And if I'm being honest with myself, I haven't either. I could have done more to try to stop Carl's behavior without losing myself, because no one deserves to be treated badly just because they have a different view from someone. Can't he just agree to disagree and call it a day?

Hmm. Whoever said "sticks and stones may break your bones, but words will never hurt you" can have several seats. The truth is that words do hurt...but they can also uplift. A person just needs to decide what they are going to do with their words.

CHAPTER 10

Nice to Meet You

THE NEXT DAY AT SCHOOL, I walk in the cafeteria for breakfast and see my friends sitting by the bay window. They spot me and wave. I salute them. I then see Michael sitting by the water fountain alone and motion to them that I'm going to head that way. Alex and Bella look confused, but Bri with her extra-ness yells out, "Yaaaaas queen!"

I mouth back at her, "Stop," and make a face, but then smile. I mean, can't I just be nice to someone without it meaning more than that?

I get to his table and ask if I can have a seat. Michael looks behind him, as if checking to see if I was talking to someone else. He realizes I am speaking to him and eagerly motions for me to have a seat. We sit in silence for a couple of minutes, only hearing the sounds of us eating and cafeteria chatter. I look down and see he's eating some Frosted Flakes. I finally decide to break the silence.

"Cereal, huh, so the eggs and bacon didn't tickle your fancy?" I ask Michael.

He smiles, and dimples appear on both cheeks. "I'm a cereal type of man," he replies.

"True, you can never go wrong with a classic," I say.

"Yup, I hear *they're grrreat!*" Michael jokes, imitating Tony the Tiger.

We both chuckle. Silence falls between us again. I look off, trying to gather the right words.

"Um...I'm sorry that some of the kids are being so mean to you. I know that sucks. Um...if you don't mind me asking...why don't you stand for the Pledge of Allegiance?"

Michael stops eating his cereal and takes a deep breath. He then looks at me and replies, "Spiritual reasons."

I start to ask him what the spiritual reasons are, but I stop myself because that would be beside the point. Instead, I just smile and nod.

"Oh, okay," I reply. "Sooo, how do you like it here compared to Florida?"

"Florida's home, so it's been hard being away from it, from all my friends, and the rest of my family..." Michael pauses and fiddles with his fingers and then continues. "I mean, it's okay, I guess. I'm definitely not in Kansas anymore," chuckles Michael as he takes a sip of his apple juice.

"Yeah, I can imagine that would be difficult. I'm a DC native, so that's all I know. To have to move across the country and start anew is actually a bit terrifying. So, considering, I think you are handling it well," I reply.

"Why did your family relocate?" I ask him.

"My mom got a promotion that brought us out this way. It's just me and my mom..." Michael pauses and looks away for a moment. "My dad passed away a few years back from a motorcycle accident. He was hit by a police vehicle that mistook him for another person they were in pursuit of..." he pauses again, and his eyes become watery. "It was ruled as an accident," Michael says, clearing his throat. "So, I'm all she got right now. And I know she felt bad about having to uproot my life, but I don't want her to stress about me, you know? She has so much on her plate right now with her new position, the last thing she needs is to have to worry about me getting into trouble at school," confesses Michael.

We sit in silence for another minute. I'm trying to think of the right words to say without putting my foot in my mouth, but I can't think of anything that feels right.

"Oh...wow...I'm so sorry to hear that. I can only imagine how difficult it has been for y'all. And I'm sure your mom is super proud of the young man you are becoming," I say.

I swear, sometimes I speak and out of nowhere, a forty-year-old woman's voice comes out.

Michael doesn't say anything. Yup, you probably should have gone with the generic *"I'm sorry for your loss"* without the extras, Melanin. Ugh.

Michael, looking down at his cereal, gives a faint smile and nods. He then turns to me and asks, "So, do you see yourself leaving DC when you get older?"

Okay, no foot in the mouth. Good, good. "Hmm...I'm not sure," I reply back. "DC is home, and it would be very weird to call any other place that, especially without my parents there. But let one of the Ivies accept me, and my bags will be packed the same day!" I say, laughing.

Michael's dimples resurface on his face.

I look up and see that Bri, Bella, and an unenthused Alex have made their way to where Michael and I are sitting. "Hey, do you mind if we join you?" Bri asks Michael.

Michael smiles and replies, "The more the merrier."

They quickly settle in. "So, catch us up on what y'all are talking about," says Alex.

"Well, pretty much how the Ivy Leagues might have a bidding war over me, but no big deal," I reply with a smirk. We all laugh.

I'm glad I took a detour today.

CHAPTER 11

I Pledge

TODAY, THE TEACHER OF THE DAY will be revealed. I get to school eager to find out who won. The crew is already gathered at my table. Alex has settled into my seat, looking really comfortable. I walk up to catch the tail end of the conversation.

"Bro, that's wild," Alex exclaims to Michael. "So, your dad was recognized by the Black Lives Matter organization as a case that needs further examination?! So rad!"

"Wait...you're black?" responds Bella.

"Oh my goodness, girl really. You know black comes in every shade. You probably have some black in you too," responds Bri.

"We are all mixing pots from our ancestors," I add in. "Those differences are actually what make us *humans*, alike."

Michael chuckles, "It's okay, I actually get that often. My mom is white, and my dad was black. And yes, I identify as black."

"Yo, that's what's up dude," replies Alex.

I detect Carl and his friends in my peripheral vision. They are already gathered and ready for their usual routine. They spot Michael and eagerly head toward him with determination in their eyes.

I stand up before they get to him. "Seriously, just stop!" I say sternly to him, as I move to stand by Michael's desk.

Carl looks surprised. His steps slow down as he takes a few more steps toward Michael and me before completely stopping.

"Well, well, it looks like we got ourselves a little Snowden lover," snipes Carl toward me.

"You know what Carl? You know my dad is a soldier, and he says everyone is entitled to their First Amendment right, the freedom of speech. Michael has the right to choose whether he says the Pledge or not. He's exercising his American freedoms, and to deny someone their American rights is *un*-American. And every time my dad gets deployed, that's what he's fighting for—our rights. So why don't you stop talking about what being an American is and start *being* an American!" I say with a fire burning in my eyes.

Carl and his friends look shocked! Carl stands silent for a moment, like he is at a loss for words. Wow, maybe he actually sees his fault.

A student nearby witnessing the disagreement starts to clap, and a few others join in as well.

Carl then smirks and replies, "Come on, guys, before Melanin starts to recite 'The Star-Spangled Banner.'"

Carl and his friends laugh and walk away.

Well, I would say I expected a little more out of him after everything was said and done, but I'm not surprised that what I said went in one ear and out the other. You can't win them all, but that doesn't mean you shouldn't try, right? And I don't know, maybe deep down somewhere he really did hear what was said and felt it. But if so, we certainly won't be seeing a change in him...at least not today. All I do know for sure is I feel proud of myself, and no one, not even Carl, can take that feeling away.

Minutes later after we get to our seats, Miss Miller enters the classroom from the hall. She looks upset. "Due to some of the unkind actions from fellow students that have been discovered, there will be no Teacher of the Day today. We will try again next week. I strongly suggest that you all take this time to reflect on what could have been done differently and make those changes," she tells the class.

The class erupts in groans. "That's not fair," calls out one classmate in dismay. "Why are we all getting in trouble? It's only *certain* students who have been mean to others," calls out another, as they side-eye Carl.

"That's enough!" Miss Miller replies. "I am aware of that, and those students will have an additional private consequence for their unkind actions. However, too many classmates took part in the bullying by laughing at what was being said and done, which further incites those ill-intended actions. And to be clear, standing by silently is also wrong. Someone could have come and told me or another adult privately if they weren't comfortable saying anything or didn't know what to do. Now please pull out your journals, as you'll be writing a five-paragraph essay about what kindness means to you."

"Yo, this is some bull!" replies Carl.

"Congratulations, Mr. Charles, for getting an automatic three before the official school day begins. I believe that's a new record. Please see me after class," responds Miss Miller to Carl.

"Ooo, you know what's up when you're hit with just the last name from a teacher. Ha! Sir you've been dismissed. Byeee," Bri attempts to whisper to our table.

"Bri!" Miss Miller calls out.

"My apologies ma'am, my apologies," replies Bri, nodding in agreement.

"So, you thought now was the time to get in one last jab," Bella whispers to Bri, shaking her head. Bri rolls her eyes and they engage in a back and forth.

I sigh, too saddened to try to mediate between them right now. I'm awfully disappointed to hear this news, but I also know that no one truly earned the award, which is meant for someone who has consistently shown their leadership skills in all the themes for the Week of Responsibility.

Miss Miller announces that it's time for the morning announcements and turns on the TV. The Pledge of Allegiance slide comes up, and the class stands to recite it. Michael stays seated. I cover my right hand over my heart and reach out to hold Michael's hand with my other.

Michael looks up and seems surprised. He gives me the biggest smile and eagerly grabs my hand.

I smile back and then face the front of the room to recite the Pledge, feeling proud to be an American, and acting like a *true* American.

Acknowledgments

FIRST, I WOULD LIKE TO THANK my mother, Jackie, who has always been my biggest supporter and taught me the value of treating people the way I wanted to be treated at an early age.

To the National Museum of African American History and Culture, thank you so much for fielding my questions and providing me with the necessary resources I needed—all images and passage quotes are credited to "Alan Karchmer/NMAAHC."

To my editing team, I could not have done this without your guidance and direction. Your feedback was invaluable for me to finish this book. To my book editor, Carey, your thoughts, ideas, and questions allowed me to evolve this story in ways I didn't even imagine. To my production editor, Lauren, I truly appreciate your dedication and patience with me and this story as it developed. Your passion for this project was undeniable and you graciously guided me through every step along the way.

To my amazingly talented illustrator, Bennie, thank you for your dedication to creating my vision. The scenes turned out better than I could have imagined.

And finally, a huge thank you to my family and friends who have supported me throughout this whole process. In particular: Tatianna, Maura, Hanna, Donovan, and Suzanne. From reading my original drafts and providing feedback, to the initial sketch ideas, to helping me network and connect with the right people—thank you for going above and beyond to support me in my first book-writing endeavor. I appreciate and value you all.

About the Author

CANDICE DAVIS is a middle school Special Education Teacher in Washington, DC, with a background in film. Candice started her career in education as a Curriculum and Personnel Specialist, writing grants and proposals. Due to her desire to have more of a direct impact with disadvantaged students, she transitioned into teaching. This is Candice's debut book. She holds a M.Ed. in Educational Psychology with a focus in Social Foundations from the University of Virginia and a BA in Film and Video Studies from George Mason University.